A NOTE TO PARENTS

Disney's First Readers Level 2 books were created for beginning readers who are gaining confidence in their early reading skills.

Compared to Level 1 books, **Level 2** books have slightly smaller type and contain more words to a page. Although sentence structure is still simple, the stories are slightly longer and more complex.

Just as children need training wheels when learning to ride a bicycle, they need the support of a good model when learning to read. Every time your child sees that you enjoy reading, whether alone or with him or her, you provide the encouragement needed to build reading confidence. Here are some helpful hints to use with the **Disney's First Readers Level 2** books:

★ Play or act out each character's words. Change your voice to indicate which character is speaking. As your child becomes comfortable with the printed text, he or she can take a favorite character's part and read those passages.

★ Have your child try reading the story. If your child asks about a word, do not interrupt the flow of reading to make him or her sound it out. Pronounce the word for your child. If, however, he or she begins to sound it out, be gently encouraging—your child is developing phonetic skills!

★ Read aloud. It's still important at this level to read to your child. With your child watching, move a finger smoothly along the text. Do not stop at each word. Change the tone of your voice to indicate punctuation marks, such as questions and exclamations. Your child will begin to notice how words and punctuation marks make sense and can make reading fun.

★ Let your child ask you questions about the story. This will help to develop your child's critical thinking skills. Use the After-Reading Fun activities provided at the end of each book as a fun exercise to further enhance your child's reading skills.

★ Praise all reading efforts warmly and often!

Remember that early-reading experiences that you share with your child can help him or her to become a confident and successful reader later on!

— Patricia Koppman
Past President
International Reading Association

To Sophie and Zachary
My very own Lady and Tramp

And in memory of Lucy and Henry

First published by Disney Press, New York, New York.
This edition published by Scholastic Inc.,
90 Old Sherman Turnpike, Danbury, Connecticut 06816
by arrangement with Disney Licensed Publishing.

SCHOLASTIC and associated logos are trademarks of Scholastic Inc.

ISBN 0-7172-6458-0

Printed in the U.S.A.

What's That Noise?

by Carol Publiano-Martin
Illustrated by Sol Studios

Disney's First Readers — Level 2
A Story from Disney's *Lady and the Tramp*

SCHOLASTIC INC.

New York   Toronto   London   Auckland   Sydney
Mexico City   New Delhi   Hong Kong   Buenos Aires

It was a dark night and the weather was wild. Lady and Tramp were alone in the house.

All of a sudden, Lady heard a noise.

"What's that noise?" Lady asked Tramp.

"It's just the floor creaking," Tramp said. "These old houses always creak."

Lady wasn't sure he was right.

But Tramp said, "Lady, we are safe and sound. I am the bravest dog around!"

Tramp shut his eyes. But Lady couldn't sleep.

"I must watch the house while everyone is out!" Lady said to herself.

Then, Lady heard another noise.
This time it sounded like a whisper.
Lady shook Tramp awake.
"What's that noise?" Lady asked.

Lady stood watch again.
She heard another noise!
Bang! Crash!
Was there someone outside
the house?

"That noise?" asked Tramp. "That is just the wind. Lady, we are safe and sound. I am the bravest dog around!"

"What's that noise?" Lady asked Tramp.

Tramp said, "That is just thunder. Lady, we are safe and sound. I am the bravest dog around!"

"I hope you are right," Lady said. "We are in charge of keeping the house safe tonight."

Plink! Plink!

Lady heard another sound. Was there someone inside the house?

Lady ran to the kitchen. She barked,
and Tramp ran in.

"What's that noise?" Lady asked.

"That is just the rain," Tramp said.
"It is falling into that pot."

Tramp said, "Lady, we are safe and sound. I am the bravest dog around!"

All of a sudden the windows began
to shake. Lady heard so many noises!
Then, she heard a loud bark.
"Ruff! Ruff! Ruff!"
It was Tramp!

Lady ran into the next room. She found Tramp on top of the piano! He was looking at a big shadow on the wall.

"What is that?" Tramp asked.

Lady knew she had to be brave. There was something in the house. She had to find out what it was.

Lady quietly walked across the floor.

"I must be brave," Lady said to herself. She looked behind the door.

It was nothing scary at all. It was a teeny, tiny bug!

Tramp was still on the piano.

"It's just a tiny bug," Lady said.
"Don't be afraid."

"Afraid? I wasn't afraid," Tramp said.
"I just wanted to make sure you were
being a good watchdog."

"Tramp, you were right all along,"
Lady said. "We are safe and sound."

"That's right," Tramp said. "We are
the *two* bravest dogs around!"

Enhance the reading experience with follow-up questions to help your child develop reading comprehension and increase his/her awareness of words.

Approach this with a sense of play. Make a game of having your child answer the questions. You do not need to ask all the questions at one time. Let these questions be fun discussions rather than a test. If your child doesn't have instant recall, encourage him/her to look back into the book to "research" the answers. You'll be modeling what good readers do and, at the same time, forging a sharing bond with your child.

What's That Noise?

1. **Where were Lady and Tramp sleeping?**

2. **Why couldn't Lady sleep?**

3. **What made the _Bang! Crash!_ noise?**

4. **What made the big, scary shadow on the wall?**

5. **Name some things that you see in the house.**

6. **Can you think of words that rhyme with "plink"?**

Answers: 1. the house. **2.** she heard a noise. **3.** the thunder. **4.** a teeny, tiny bug. **5.** _possible answers:_ chair, pillow, rugs, plant, fish bowl, bird cage, curtains, piano. **6.** _possible answers:_ drink, rink, think, sink, link, mink, pink, stink, wink.